The Dinosaur Who Asked "What for?"

Russell Punter

Illustrated by Andy Elkerton

The Explorer Club is off to camp.

But Daisy's feeling lazy.

"Hurry, Daisy," mutters Sid,
as he waits by the door.

But Daisy drags her bag along
and loudly moans...

They reach the camp.

But Daisy rests upon her tent and loudly groans...

"We need some wood to build a fire."
Bob scans the forest floor.

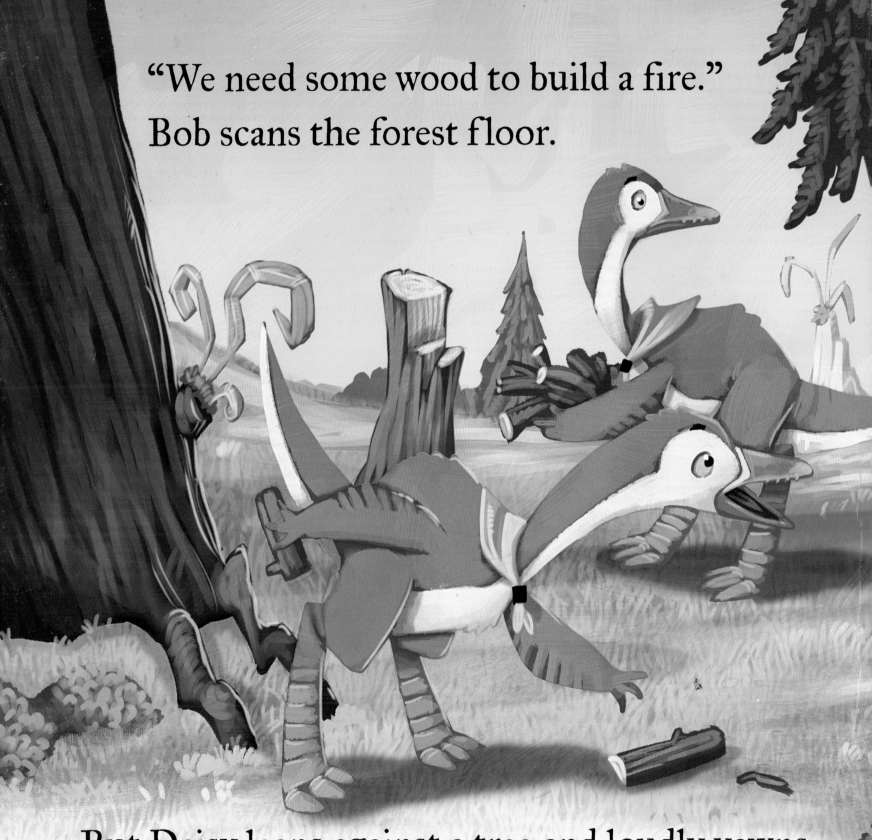

But Daisy leans against a tree and loudly yawns...

"Let's all get water," Maisie says.
"Please line up and I'll pour."

Daisy flops down on a log
and loudly wails...

Split! Splat! It's raining. Daisy frowns.
Her tent's still on the floor.

"I should have put it up at once.
And now I know...

She fills a bucket from the well.

Will one be quite enough?

She fills up two,

three,

four and more...

until she's out of puff.

She turns back to the site.

A spark has made a tent catch fire.

Daisy shouts out, "Follow me!"

"Grab these buckets!" Daisy cries.

They quickly take a bucket each...
and race back to the tents.

"Let me serve it," Daisy says.
"Please sit down, be my guests."

"Hey, you've saved the camp," says Sid.
"You've earned a little rest."

"What, go back to my lazy ways?
Just as I was before?"

Daisy simply gives a grin
and loudly roars...

Edited by Jenny Tyler and Lesley Sims

This edition first published in 2023 by Usborne Publishing Ltd., Usborne House,
83-85 Saffron Hill, London EC1N 8RT, England. usborne.com Copyright © 2023, 2021 Usborne Publishing Ltd.